WENDY HARMER

Illustrated by Gypsy Taylor

RANDOM HOUSE AUSTRALIA

For Maevie, my very own cherry blossom

A Random House book
Published by Random House Australia Pty Ltd
Level 3, 100 Pacific Highway, North Sydney NSW 2060
www.randomhouse.com.au

First published by Random House Australia in 2010
Copyright © Out of Harms Way Pty Ltd 2010

National Library of Australia
Cataloguing-in-Publication Entry

Harmer, Wendy
Pearlie and the cherry blossom fairy / Wendy Harmer; illustrator Gypsy Taylor
ISBN: 978 1 74166 378 5
Series: Harmer, Wendy, Pearlie, the park fairy; 12
Target audience: For primary school age
Subjects: Fairies – Juvenile fiction
Other authors/contributors: Taylor, Gypsy

A823.3

Designed and typeset by Jobi Murphy
Printed and bound by Everbest Printing Co.Ltd, China

It was springtime in Japan when Pearlie the
Park Fairy flew over the old city of Kyoto,
and the famous cherry trees were in bloom.

'Buds and blossoms! Everything is pink,'
Pearlie sighed happily. 'The whole of this park
is perfectly pink!'

When Pearlie was named 'Fairy of the Year', she had left her home in Jubilee Park to visit all the other Park Fairies in the world. What a life it must be, she thought, to live here in the flowering cherry trees of Japan!

She waved goodbye to Queen Emerald's magic ladybird and it flew off through clouds of rosy petals.

'Konichiwa!'

Pearlie turned to see an elegant fairy dressed
in a gloriously embroidered silk gown.

'My name is Akiko,' she said as she bowed low.
'Welcome to the Park of the Imperial Palace.
Will you have some tea?'

'Yes, please,' Pearlie replied.

Akiko lived in an old lantern carved from stone.
Its roof was covered in soft green moss.

'Oooh, it's lovely,' said Pearlie.

'It's very cosy when the snow comes,' Akiko
smiled. 'Please leave your boots by the door.'
Pearlie was very pleased she had worn her
best frilly socks!

She sat at a low table and Akiko served
a delicious breakfast of tiny sugary cakes
and a bowl of hot green tea.

'Thank you,' said Pearlie.

'In Japan we say "*arigato*",' said Akiko.

Everything sounded very strange to Pearlie.
She had never met a Japanese fairy before,
and had so many questions to ask. She learned
that Akiko's lovely dress was called a '*kimono*'
and that '*konichiwa*' meant 'hello'.

'My job is to care for all the cherry trees – the *sakura* – in the park,' said Akiko. 'I sing to them and let them know spring is coming. It's very important that the *sakura* make a lovely display.'

Pearlie nodded. At home in Jubilee Park she was always very proud when the roses looked their best.

'Soon the park will be crowded with visitors who come to see the flowers,' said Akiko. 'And my home is the perfect place to watch all the parties from without being seen.'

Pearlie and Akiko peeked out of the old stone lantern. All morning families and friends came by to spread picnic blankets under the trees. They ate, played games, strolled by the pond and took lots of photographs of the branches heavy with blossoms.

'Everyone in Kyoto loves cherry blossom time!' declared Akiko.

'Look!' cried Pearlie as she pointed with her wand. 'That flower is moving all by itself.'

Akiko giggled. 'Hee, hee! That's a paper umbrella and under it is my friend Yuki. He is helping himself to the picnic treats.'

Pearlie looked again, and sure enough, there was
a mouse carrying away a whole tea cake.

'I hope Yuki's hungry,' laughed Pearlie. 'That's
a whopping cake for a very small mouse!'

Rumble!

The two fairies were startled to hear thunder. The sun disappeared behind towers of black clouds.

'It's a spring storm!' shouted Akiko. Pearlie pulled her wings tightly around her. She didn't like storms. In the next moment, huge hailstones came smashing down.

All over the park the visitors grabbed their picnic blankets and their bats and balls. They ran for the gates as fast as their legs could go.

'*Tasukete kudasai!*' they shrieked.

'They're calling for help,' cried Akiko over the deafening noise of hailstones on the roof of the lantern.

"Aiee, aieee!" came a terrified voice.

Pearlie and Akiko looked out and there was Yuki! He was holding his paper umbrella and being blown high into the sky. Giant balls of ice battered the cherry trees. The wind howled and the air was filled with swirling petals.

Bang!

A mighty hailstone hit the roof of the old stone lantern.

Crack!

Suddenly it was split right down the middle! Huge hailstones pelted onto the floor and a freezing wind whipped through the lantern. Pearlie and Akiko gripped the edge of the front door and watched as Akiko's kimonos and furniture were all picked up and whisked away, out of sight.

'Hurly-burly!' shouted Pearlie.

And then, just as quickly as it had started, the storm stopped.

The sun peeped out from behind the clouds and Pearlie and Akiko looked out from their hiding place. They were amazed to see that every single cherry tree was as bare as could be! All the blossoms had been torn from the branches and were lying in a thick pink carpet on the ground.

'This is terrible!' wailed Akiko. 'And where is my friend Yuki?'

'Aiee, aieeee!' the voice came again.

Pearlie spotted a tiny figure clinging to the roof of the Imperial Palace. 'There he is!' exclaimed Pearlie. 'We'll go and help him. Quickly, let's find our wands.'

But Pearlie and Akiko could not find them. The lantern was perfectly bare. Their wands had been blown away across the park, along with everything else.

'We'll have to fly Yuki down instead' said Pearlie, and she whizzed off with a very soggy Akiko after her.

High up on top of the palace roof, Yuki the mouse was shaking with fright. 'Eeek, eek,' he squealed. 'Please help me!'

Akiko held Yuki's shivering paw. 'This is my new friend Pearlie,' she said. 'We will get you down.'

'Take our hands!' said Pearlie.

The two fairies tried very hard to lift Yuki, but sadly, the little mouse had eaten one too many tea cakes. He was just too heavy!

'Eeeyah!' sobbed Yuki.

'What will we do now?' wailed Akiko.

Then Pearlie had a very good idea. 'You go and find Yuki's umbrella,' she said to Akiko. 'I've got work to do.'

Pearlie flew down to the grass and began
to pick up the fallen cherry blossom petals.
It was hard work without her wand, but
soon enough she had pushed them
into a great big pile.

'YUKI! WAIT UNTIL A BREEZE
COMES, HOLD YOUR UMBRELLA
HIGH, AND THEN ...
JUMP!' Pearlie called.

Just then a soft wind sang through the branches of the cherry trees.

'NOW!' shouted Pearlie.

Yuki leapt from the roof holding his paper umbrella. It was a bit ragged from the storm, but still strong enough to hold him. The breeze blew Yuki this way and that. Down and down he floated with Akiko flying close behind.

WHUMP!

Yuki landed safely in the soft pink petals.

'Hooray!' cried Akiko as she clapped her tiny hands.

Yuki climbed from the petals and bowed very
low. '*Arigato*, honourable friend Pearlie,' he
squeaked. 'How may I assist you?'

'Well,' Pearlie replied thoughtfully, 'could you
help us find our wands?'

'*Hai!*' agreed Yuki and he scurried off.

Akiko looked at her broken lantern. 'I'll have to find a new place to live,' she said sadly.

'There are so many lovely lanterns in the park,' said Pearlie. 'It might be fun to have a new house for the spring and summer.'

'Why, yes it would,' agreed Akiko.

Pearlie and Akiko spent the afternoon house-hunting in the Imperial Park. They looked at many, *many* lanterns. Some were made of stone and others of paper. Some were too roomy and others too small.

Then they spied a beautiful wooden
one painted as red as cherries.

'Oooh, it's perfect!' said Akiko.

At that moment, Yuki came scampering across the scattered pink petals. He held a precious fairy wand in each paw.

Pearlie and Akiko were very glad to see them. 'Thank you! *Arigato!*' they cheered.

Yuki bowed once more, very pleased to have been of service. 'I saw all of Akiko's furniture too,' he puffed. 'But I'm afraid all her pretty kimonos landed in the pond and have been nibbled by the golden carp.'

'Fish and frocks!' gasped Pearlie.

'Hee, hee, hee,' giggled Akiko. 'It does not matter. I can surely make new ones.'

Pearlie zoomed off to look for Akiko's furniture.
She found her bed in a bush and her teapot up
a tree! Pearlie was thrilled and used her magic to
zap Akiko's belongings into her new home.

Akiko got to work too. The clever little fairy
gathered an armful of petals and found her
sewing kit full of pins and needles and beautiful
silk threads.

That evening in the lovely new lantern, Pearlie and Akiko feasted on blossom buns, petal sushi and cherry fizz that Yuki had made.

Then Akiko modelled her petal *kimonos,* all handmade in shades from deepest rose to snowy white. She had collected moss and leaves to make shawls and wide *obi* belts.

'You are the prettiest fairy in all Japan,' sighed Pearlie.

'*Hai!*' Yuki agreed.

In the days that followed, Pearlie met all the creatures that lived in the Imperial Park. She rode on the backs of the tortoises, swam with the golden carp and played hide-and-seek with the dragonflies.

When the cherry trees were at last covered
in bright new leaves, Pearlie knew it was time
for her to go. Queen Emerald's ladybird soon
arrived to take her away.

Akiko offered Pearlie a small gift tied with
scarlet ribbon. 'I will never forget you,' she said.
'Every time the cherry trees are covered with
buds, I will think of Pearlie the Park Fairy.'

'And I will think of you too,' said Pearlie. 'When
spring comes to Jubilee Park and the golden
flowers burst on the wattle trees, I'll remember
cherry blossom time in Japan.'

Pearlie bowed to her new friends.

'*Sayonara!*' said Akiko and Yuki. 'That means "goodbye".'

'But not forever,' said Pearlie as she kissed them both.

Pearlie jumped on board the ladybird and it took to the sky. She heard Akiko's voice calling through the bare branches: 'Nothing is forever. Not even the famous cherry blossoms of Kyoto.'

Pearlie unwrapped her gift and found a small pearl that had been gathered from an oyster shell in the Imperial Pond. She sniffed back a little tear and then she smiled – she was off, looking forward to her next adventure.